TODAY AT THE BLUEBIRD CAFÉ

Remembering my dad, Bruce Glezen,
who loved a good rhyme—D. R.

To Jenny and Dieter—thank you for
all the years of help and friendship.—J. R.

Margaret K. McElderry Books
An imprint of Simon & Schuster Children's Publishing Division
1230 Avenue of the Americas, New York, New York 10020
Text copyright © 2007 by Deborah Ruddell
Illustrations copyright © 2007 by Joan Rankin
Book design by Ann Bobco
The text for this book is set in Celestia Antiqua.
The illustrations for this book are rendered in watercolor.
Manufactured in China
10 9 8 7 6 5 4 3 2 1
Library of Congress Cataloging-in-Publication Data
Ruddell, Deborah.
Today at the bluebird café : a branchful of birds / Deborah Ruddell ;
illustrated by Joan Rankin.—1st ed.
p. cm.
ISBN-13: 978-0-689-87153-5
ISBN-10: 0-689-87153-8
1. Birds—Juvenile poetry. 2. Children's poetry, American.
I. Rankin, Joan, ill. II. Title.
PS3618.U236B73 2007
811'.54—dc22
2005028561

FIRST
EDITION

TODAY AT THE BLUEBIRD CAFÉ

a branchful of birds

DEBORAH RUDDELL

JOAN RANKIN

MARGARET K. McELDERRY BOOKS
New York · London · Toronto · Sydney

TODAY AT THE BLUEBIRD CAFÉ

It's all-you-can-eat at the Bluebird Café,
a grasshopper-katydid-cricket buffet,
with berries and snails and a bluebottle fly,
a sip of the lake and a bite of the sky.

THE LOON'S LAUGH

No tweedle-dee-dee on your windowsill.
No sunshiny tune from the top of a hill.
No chirp. No coo. No warble or cheep.
No bubbly twitter or sweet little peep.
The kind of a laugh in the purple of night
that makes you sit up and turn on the light.
A wail. A chuckle. A shriek at the moon.
You pull up your covers. You *hope* it's a loon.

THE CARDINAL

Stoplights and cherries
and roses and berries,
a ruby, a wagon,
a flame from a dragon;
crimson-vermilion,
a sunset Brazilian,
the tip of his tail,
the cap on his head:
valentineSantaClaustotallyred.

THE EAGLE

She rides the sky like she owns the sun,
on a sea of air and light—
surfing, skimming, rising high,
then sweeping low and tight.

She swoops to catch a perfect wave,
her wings held straight and true.
You lift your chin and hold your breath
and *wish* you could do it too.

THE WOODPECKER

If you think that his life is a picnic,
a seesawing day at the park,
I ask you *just once* to consider
the aftertaste
of bark.

HUMMINGBIRD SEARCH

If you spy a greedy bird
who's the size of your thumb
and he's covered all in sequins
and you hear him hum
and he helicopters down
to the honeysuckle vine
and he takes a big swig
from the columbine
and he flaps his teeny wings
like a maniac,
would you tell him that I miss him
and to please come back?

TOUCAN TOUR GUIDE

I was touring Peru in a silver canoe,
and my guide was a toucan named Zeke—
a talkative fellow with splashes of yellow
and green on his eye-catching beak.

The river was cold, the sunlight was gold,
we were feeling as free as could be . . .
when something I said made Zeke turn his head,
and the tip of his beak hit a tree.

So we stopped for the night at a vine-covered site,
and Zeke made a fire by our tent.
I tried not to peek at his curious beak,
but to tell you the truth, it was bent.

GOOD OLD PUFFIN

Good old puffin holds her ground
while bitter breezes swirl around
her lonely, frozen lookout place
and sting her sober, chalky face.

When midnight comes, it starts to sleet
and blocks of ice surround her feet.
Beside her rests her cocoa cup.
Now grab it, puffin! Drink it up!

A VULTURE'S GUIDE TO GOOD MANNERS

I never never never
put my elbows on the table,
and my face will never show it
if my tummy feels unstable.

I never tell a story
when my beak is full of food,
or eat a sprig of broccoli
that hasn't been well chewed.

I never leave the table
until I've been excused.
When someone breaks the gravy boat,
I never act amused.

I never spit my food out.
I'm never ever late.
But when I come to dinner,
I *always* clean my plate.

HOOPOE VOODOO*

You people who pooh-pooh the hoopoe
are taking a horrible chance:
He's likely to soothe you with voodoo
and stew you with quite a few ants.

*"Hoopoe" is pronounced as HOO-poo.

MRS. CROW GETS DRESSED

She gives her satin coat a shake
and buffs her leather nose;
she tries to pull the wrinkles
from her charcoal panty hose.

She finds her purse and fills it up
with candy corn and straw;
she bends her knees and pushes off
with a gravel-throated "Caw!"

THERE'S A ROBIN
IN THE BATHROOM

He sings in the shower
and bathes in the sink.
He lounges in bubbles
to help himself think.
He leaves little footprints
on top of my soap.
I'd *like* to go in,
but I'm giving up hope.

He uses my toothbrush
to scour his wings.
He sloshes and splashes
on all of our things.
He sprinkles himself
in my mother's cologne.
He asks me politely
to leave him alone.

BLUE JAY BLUES

Blue as a bruise
on a swollen knee,
ruling the world
from a maple tree.

Squawking out orders,
getting his way,
hogging the feeder,
and having his say.

Raising a fuss,
causing a flap,
a flying complainer
in need of a nap.

MOCKINGBIRD WARNING

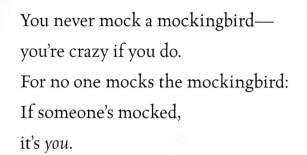

You never mock a mockingbird—
you're crazy if you do.
For no one mocks the mockingbird:
If someone's mocked,
it's *you*.

THE KINGFISHER

I'm the boss of the marsh,
where the winters are harsh,
the high-flyin' king of my home.
I don't give a care
for the state of my hair,
and I won't use a brush or a comb.

When I set out to fish
for a rib-stickin' dish,
I dive like a blue-streakin' flash.
I cut through the air
with a natural flair,
and all you can see is my splash.

BYE-BYE, IBIS

Our pointy-beaked ibis
stopped by to remind us
today is the day she must fly.
"I miss my big sister,"
she said when we quizzed her,
and pointed her wing to the sky.
She sniffed the hibiscus
and cautiously kissed us
good-bye, and we tried not to cry.

THE QUAIL

A certain bird
is so refined,
so brainy and smart and well-read,
that every time
he thinks a thought,
a comma pops out of his head.

THE GREAT
HORNED OWL

He's motionless and silent
like a stuck-up king in a play—
his puffed-up chest in a fancy vest
and a robe of gold and gray.

And you really have to admire him,
perched in a statuelike stance,
with his regal air and his royal stare
and his snug-fitting feather pants.

THE COCKATOO

She reminds me of one of those wedding cakes
with frosting swoops and coconut flakes.
Pure vanilla, tall and proud,
guaranteed to draw a crowd.
And on her head with a bird's-eye view—
a sugar-coated curlicue.

BRAVO, BOBOLINK!

All by himself
on a lily-pad stage,
a bobolink warbled away.
After he finished,
a beetle applauded
and gave him a clover bouquet.

THE SWAN

Fairy-tale bird on a moonlit pond,
pulled by stars or a magic wand
through lily pads and wonderlands
of castle moats and pixie clans,

missing shoes and midnight chimes,
ogres, toads, and nursery rhymes,
lessons learned and broken wings,
wishes, wolves, and flower kings.

PENGUIN'S LULLABY

For you, dear sleepy penguin,
we'll sing a lullaby
of ostriches and emus
who sail around the sky.
We'll smooth your icy pillow.
We'll keep you safe and dry.
You'll dream about tomorrow,
and in your dreams
you'll fly.